The Floating Forest

STRIPES PUBLISHING LIMITED
An imprint of the Little Tiger Group
1 Coda Studios, 189 Munster Road,
London SW6 6AW

A paperback original
First published in Great Britain in 2020

Text copyright © Linda Chapman, 2020
Illustrations © Mirelle Ortega, 2020

ISBN: 978-1-78895-195-1

The right of Linda Chapman to be identified as the author and Mirelle Ortega as the
illustrator of this work respectively has been asserted by them
in accordance with the Copyright, Designs and Patents Act, 1988.

Printed and bound in the UK.

The Forest Stewardship Council® (FSC®) is a global, not-for-profit organization
dedicated to the promotion of responsible forest management worldwide. FSC defines
standards based on agreed principles for responsible forest stewardship that are supported
by environmental, social, and economic stakeholders. To learn more, visit www.fsc.org

2 4 6 8 10 9 7 5 3 1

MERMAIDS ROCK

The Floating Forest

Linda Chapman
Illustrated by Mirelle Ortega

LITTLE TIGER

LONDON

Contents

Welcome to Mermaids Rock!

Marina
& Sami

Kai & Tommy

Naya & Octavia

Coralie & Dash

Luna & Melly

Chapter One
Playing Dares

Coralie stared at the magic whirlpool as it swirled round the base of Mermaids Rock – a huge, submerged rock shaped like a mermaid's tail that jutted up from the seabed. "Kai's been gone ages," she said to the two mergirls swimming beside her. "I wonder where he is."

Naya looked anxious. "I hope he hasn't got into trouble." Octavia, Naya's pet octopus, hid her face behind her arms at the thought.

"He's probably ended up somewhere really fun," said Marina confidently. "I bet he'll be back soon."

Coralie pushed her wavy dark-red hair back from her face. She hoped Marina was right.

Mermaids Rock marked the entrance to the merpeople's shallow-water coral reef, and the magic whirlpool could transport them to any ocean in the world. Usually, there were merguards near it, watching the ocean beyond Mermaids Rock for anything that might threaten the reef. However, the water was very calm at the moment, and there had been no report of any dangerous creatures, so the guards were only stopping by every few hours.

Seeing that the rock was unguarded, Coralie had decided it would be really fun if she and her friends dared each other to dive into the whirlpool without saying a destination and see where they ended up. They had waited until the guards had done their early-afternoon check and then the game had begun!

Marina had gone first and had been

2

transported to Australia's Great Barrier Reef, swimming with giant manta rays. Naya had plunged in next and found herself among a school of playful porpoises off the coast of Norway. Then it had been Kai's turn.

Coralie's pet dolphin, Dash, clicked his tongue and swam closer to the whirlpool. The water was starting to swirl faster, turning into frothy white foam.

"This could be Kai coming back now," said Marina, excited.

"It is!" gasped Coralie as a merboy with thick black hair and a red tail shot out of the magical whirlpool, closely followed by a large hawksbill turtle. The two of them catapulted up through the water. Kai turned a somersault and dived back down to meet them with Tommy close behind him.

"You're back!" said Naya, hugging Kai in relief. "We were getting worried."

Kai grinned. "Sorry – I lost track of time."

"I said you'd just be having too much fun," said Marina. "Where did you end up?"

"In the Bering Sea. It was freezing but we saw a young polar bear!" said Kai. "It was following a seal and at first I thought it might chase us, but it didn't. It came over and let me pat it. Then we went swimming with it until we got too cold and came back."

"Oh wow!" breathed Marina, Coralie and

Naya. All four of them loved animals and they had formed a group called the Save the Sea Creatures Club to help any animals that were in trouble.

Coralie chuckled. "Sounds like you had a *beary* good time, Kai."

Her friends groaned and Octavia clapped her arms over her ears.

"What?" Coralie innocently. "Are you trying to tell me you can't *bear* my jokes?"

She ducked as the others grabbed handfuls of seaweed and threw them at her. Dash whistled as if he was laughing. Coralie giggled. "Come on, Dash. It's our turn to go into the whirlpool now." Her tummy fizzed with excitement. Where would they end up? It could be anywhere in the world!

"Have fun!" called Marina.

"But don't be longer than ten minutes or we'll come after you," warned Naya.

Coralie adjusted her seaweed satchel that

5

she wore across her body and plunged into the whirlpool with Dash beside her. It was like diving into a rainbow! Bright colours flashed around them. They spun round and round until Coralie started to feel dizzy. Then the colours cleared and she saw that she was in a bluey-green world with strange floating trees that seemed to be made out of seaweed. The seaweed was growing up from the rocks on the ocean floor, the strands of it twisting together to form thick, flexible trunks, topped near the surface by canopies of ribbon-like fronds that waved in the current. Shafts of sunlight shone down through the water, illuminating the turquoise depths. It felt serene and peaceful – a safe, hidden world.

"I wonder where we are," Coralie said to Dash. She'd never been anywhere like this strange, beautiful forest and the water felt much colder than she was used to. She jumped as she suddenly spotted two sleek grey seals.

"Dash, look!" she said. Seals didn't live on the warm tropical reef where the merpeople had their home. The seals stared curiously at Dash and Coralie before moving on.

There was another flurry of movement from above and a little brown sea otter came swimming down from the surface. He plucked a spiny purple sea urchin from the rocks on the bottom with his paws, gave them a cheeky wink and then swam back up.

"This place is awesome!" Coralie said to Dash. "Let's explore." A small whirlpool was swirling just a few tail-lengths away from her. "We must remember where this whirlpool is though," she told Dash. "It's our way home. You'll have to help me get back here!"

Dash nodded. Like all dolphins, he was very good at remembering things and he never got lost. "Come on then!" said Coralie playfully. Flicking her purple tail fin, she set off through the trees. They swam over a bed of pink sea urchins and passed two lobsters having a fight on a rock. A dark grey bat ray, with flat, wide wings and a long, thin tail, was swimming along the bottom, digging in the patches of sand for krill. Then she spotted a mottled brown moray eel hiding in a crack between two boulders, its pale eyes gleaming.

As Coralie swam over to get a better look, she saw something shiny half buried in some kelp fronds. Diving down, she realized it was a bottle and she pulled it out. It looked old – its sides were dull and pitted with marks, and a cork was plugged firmly into its neck. There was a rolled-up piece of paper inside which seemed to have writing and drawings on it. "There's a message in here, Dash," she said curiously. "I wonder what it says."

Dash peered over her shoulder.

Coralie tried to get the cork out, but it was wedged in really tightly. Glancing around to see if she could find a sharp razor-clam shell to help her get it out, she caught sight of a young sea lion peeping at her from behind a rock. It was so cute that she gave up on opening the bottle and stuffed it into her satchel instead. "A sea lion!" she exclaimed, pointing. "Over there, Dash!"

The young sea lion was dark brown with paler circles round its huge eyes. The long whiskers on its muzzle trembled inquisitively as it watched them. "Hey there," Coralie called softly, holding out her hand. "Come and say hello. I won't hurt you." She wished she was like her younger cousin, Luna, who had an amazing knack with sea creatures. They all instantly loved her and would come straight to her.

Dash whistled a greeting and the sea lion edged out from behind the rock. It nudged Dash with its nose, then shot backwards as if shocked by its own bravery and hid behind the rock again. Coralie giggled.

Her laughter seemed to relax the youngster.

He made a barking noise before swimming out. When Dash gently nuzzled him, he raced away in excitement, gliding in a circle round them.

"You're gorgeous," Coralie said.

The sea lion rubbed his head against her hand, making a clicking noise with his tongue a bit like Dash sometimes did.

Dash looked back the way they had come, flapped his flippers and chattered his teeth anxiously.

"You're right," Coralie said to him. "The others will be worried if we stay here much longer. We should probably go back now."

She said a reluctant goodbye to the young sea lion, who disappeared into the seaweed trees, then she followed Dash to the whirlpool. "Mermaids Rock!" she called as they dived in. She couldn't wait to tell the others about the completely *fin-credible* things she had seen!

Chapter Two
Message in a Bottle

Coralie shot out of the whirlpool. She turned head over tail and swam down to where the others were waiting impatiently. "Where did you go?" Naya asked eagerly.

Coralie's green eyes shone. "I went to the best place. I've no idea where it was, but it was some kind of underwater forest. The water was quite cold and there were these trees made of seaweed."

Marina plucked something from Coralie's thick, wavy hair. "Were they made of this type of seaweed?" she said, holding up the frond.

"Yes, do you know what it is?" Coralie asked. Marina's dad was a marine scientist and she had travelled to lots of different places with him before they had come to live at Mermaids Rock a month ago.

Marina nodded. "It's called kelp and it grows in cool, shallow water near coastlines. The trees in a kelp forest are not like the ones on land because they don't have roots. It's so cool – the kelp sticks itself to rocks and then grows upwards!"

"I've read about kelp forests," said Naya, looking animated. She loved anything to do with science. "They're important ecosystems. All sorts of fish and sea creatures live in them and marine mammals like seals and whales take their youngsters there to shelter from dangerous predators and storms." She took the frond from Marina. "Sea kelp can be used for lots of things because it's very rich in nutrients."

13

"The best thing about the forest was all the creatures. We saw seals, an otter and the cutest sea lion pup," said Coralie. "It was completely *krill-iant*, wasn't it, Dash?"

He whistled his agreement and clapped his front flippers.

"I want to go!" said Marina. "Maybe we should ask the whirlpool to take us there."

"Ooh yes!" Naya gasped. "I'd really like to collect some kelp so I can do some experiments with it."

"I want to see sea lions, seals and otters," said Kai. "And an underwater forest!"

Tommy swam up and shook his head.

Kai sighed. "Tommy's right. There probably isn't enough time now. The guards will be back for the late-afternoon inspection soon and my mum's expecting us home for tea."

"How about we go tomorrow?" suggested Coralie.

"Definitely!" said Marina.

"We can ask our parents for packed lunches and have a picnic. Let's tell them we're going out exploring for the day," said Coralie. "Hopefully they won't ask where!"

"We should see if Luna wants to come too," said Naya, nodding eagerly. Coralie's younger cousin Luna was also part of their club. She had been helping her mum at the Marine Sanctuary that day, where she could use her special skills with animals to keep them calm and make them feel better. Being younger than the others, Luna wasn't allowed to do quite as much as they were, but they tried to include her whenever they could.

"Good plan," said Marina. "She'll love the creatures in the forest."

"And they'll love her." Coralie grinned.

As they swam back to Kai's cave, gliding past the banks of colourful coral and massive orange-and-purple sea fans, Coralie remembered something. "Hey! Look what else I found while I was there." She pulled the bottle out of her satchel.

Kai took the bottle, tilting it this way and that. "It looks like there's a message written on the paper."

"I tried to read it but the cork's stuck," said Coralie.

"It could be instructions for something," Naya suggested.

"Or a secret," Kai gasped. "Maybe a note in code written by a pirate from long ago!"

Marina's eyes shone. "This could be the start

of a brand-new adventure!"

"I hope so," said Coralie. "Our last adventure was totally *fin-tastic!*"

A few weeks ago, something mysterious had been destroying the deep-water reef. Chief Razeem, the head of the merguards, had thought it was whale sharks and had sent the guards to chase them away, but Marina hadn't been so sure. She and the others had finally solved the mystery, saved the day and had also managed to help rescue a very rare sea creature at the same time!

Kai flicked his tail in excitement. "As soon as we get back to mine, I vote we get the cork out and see what the message says!"

The reef where the merpeople lived was in a remote part of the ocean that humans never visited. It stretched for miles – a beautiful underwater world of rainbow-coloured coral, waving, flower-like anemones, delicate sea fans and tall, bright sea sponges. The merpeople lived in coral caves, sharing the reef with thousands of fish and a host of other friendly sea creatures like turtles, dolphins and manatees.

Shoals of brightly coloured blue-and-yellow fish whizzed past Coralie and her friends in the turquoise water. Orange crabs scuttled across the sandy floor and tiny, shrimp-like krill bobbed around in the seaweed, trying to avoid being eaten by bigger creatures.

The gang stopped at Coralie's aunt and uncle's cave to pick up Luna who was coming to Kai's for tea, along with her manatee, Melly. Melly had a round grey body, a friendly smile and widely spaced dark eyes that twinkled with kindness. She was the largest of all the pets but she was also the gentlest.

As they swam to the cave where Kai lived with his mum, Indra, Coralie told Luna everything that had happened.

"The kelp forest sounds awesome!" Luna said longingly. "I wish I could have seen all of those amazing creatures!"

"You can come with us tomorrow if you want," said Coralie.

"I'll ask Mum and Dad tonight!" Luna said as they reached Kai's cave.

"OK, but don't say we're playing in the whirlpool," warned Coralie. "If our parents find out, they're bound to tell us we're not allowed to. Just say we're going out exploring."

Luna nodded, her eyes shining at the thought of so much fun.

They reached Kai's home.

Like most of the caves where the merpeople lived, it had a large central living space with a pot of magical, flickering green mermaid fire in the middle. The merpeople used mermaid fire for cooking and for light, but also to make mermaid powder, a substance that could add magic to many things.

There were two bedrooms leading off from the main cave – one for Kai's mum and one that Kai and Tommy shared. A kitchen area was built into one wall of the cave with shelves of carefully stacked pots and plates and, in the main cave, there were six circular blue sponges to sit on around a low table. Kai's mum's weapons – two tridents and a harpoon – were locked away in a case made from a giant clamshell by the entrance.

Kai's mum was part
of the merguards, a
group of mermaids and
mermen who protected
the reef from dangerous
predators like killer
whales and great white
sharks.

"I was just wondering
where you lot were," Indra
called from the kitchen as the
friends swam in. She had shoulder-
length black hair which she sometimes tied
back neatly in a bun when she was working,
but now she wore it loose. "What have you
been up to?"

"Oh, just this and that," said Kai vaguely.
"Playing games and looking at animals."

Luckily, his mum didn't question them
further. "Well, tea should be ready in about
fifteen minutes."

"OK, we'll go to my room until then," said Kai.

"Unless you need any help?" Marina offered politely.

"No, everything's under control, thanks, Marina," said Indra. "I saw your dad earlier by the way. He seems very excited about the coelacanth he's been studying on the deep reef."

"Yes, coelacanth are really rare – he didn't expect to find one so soon!" said Marina. She and the others had been responsible for discovering the coelacanth that her dad was studying. "She's just laid some eggs. It's incredible!"

"I definitely want to swim out and see the babies when they hatch," said Indra. "Wouldn't it be wonderful if the deep reef became a breeding ground for them?"

"That would be *foam-azing*!" said Naya.

They swam to Kai's bedroom and Coralie

took the mysterious bottle out of her seaweed satchel. "Right. How do we get this cork out?"

"Maybe we could use something to push it down inside the bottle," said Marina.

"But then the cork might block the paper," Naya pointed out. She studied the cork. "What we need is a screw, a screwdriver and a hammer. Has your mum got a toolkit, Kai?"

He nodded. "I'll get it."

He returned a few minutes later with a box full of tools. They watched as Naya used the screwdriver to put a screw into the centre of the cork. When there was just a little bit of the screw still poking up, she hooked the claw of the hammer round it and pulled hard. The cork popped out. "There we go!" said Naya, handing the bottle to Coralie.

Coralie tipped the bottle upside down and shook it vigorously, but the roll of paper was too wide to fit through the neck of the bottle.

"It won't come out!" she complained.

Naya grinned. "You're so impatient! Give it to me." She took some long-nosed, pointy pliers and used them to gently pull the piece of paper to the top of the bottle. Then she eased it out with her fingers, centimetre by centimetre. "Got it! Here we go!" She unrolled the paper and they gathered round, peering at it.

There were four drawings on the piece of paper – a rock that had a large hole in it; a cluster of stars; a sea lion's head; and a large X beside some words written in small, faded writing.

"What do they say?" Luna said. She bent closer, her long dark red hair falling over the map as she tried to read them. "It's a rhyme. It says…" She broke off with an excited yelp. "Treasure!" she exclaimed, her eyes wide. "Listen, everyone!" She read the words out loud.

Treasure in the kelp,
beyond where otters feed,
Seek a rock with a hole,
head east into the trees,
Past a galaxy of stars
then on to sea lion rock,
Underneath the rookery,
X marks the spot.

"It's a treasure map!" gasped Coralie.

Dash whistled and Melly squeaked. Caught up in the excitement, Tommy waved his flippers and Octavia and Sami zoomed round the room.

"We're going to be treasure hunters!" Marina whooped, high-fiving Coralie.

"I wonder what the treasure is," said Kai. "It could be a stack of gold bars that were stolen by a one-eyed pirate or –" his eyes grew wider – "huge chests of jewels that once belonged to a fierce king, or diamonds stolen from a dragon's lair!"

"I don't care if it's only one necklace," declared Naya. "It'll just be fun following the clues and finding it!"

"Do you think it will be dangerous?" asked Luna.

"No. The kelp forest isn't scary," Coralie reassured her. "It's a really safe place."

"Wait a moment," said Naya, frowning.

27

"What about the rule that, if anyone finds treasure in the ocean, they have to give it to the merguards so they can put it in the museum where everyone can look at it? Do you think we should tell a grown-up about this?"

"No, no, no!" said Coralie hurriedly. "If we do that, then the grown-ups will go to the kelp forest and look for it themselves."

"Please let's not tell," begged Marina. "We're not going to keep the treasure – if we do find anything, we'll give it to the guards like we should." She grinned. "But we will do the searching. It'll be so much fun!"

"Yes, let's find it ourselves!" Naya agreed, her sensible expression vanishing and an excited smile lighting up her face.

Marina beamed. "So tomorrow we go on a treasure hunt!"

Coralie chuckled as a joke popped into her head. "You know what?" she said. "If a hermit crab found this treasure, I bet he wouldn't share it."

"Why not?" asked Kai, puzzled.

"Because hermit crabs are a little *shell*fish!" Coralie said.

The others flicked water at her with their tails. Coralie giggled and dodged out of the way. She felt fizzy inside. Tomorrow they were going treasure hunting! What would they find?

Chapter Three
A New Adventure

The next morning Coralie raced to meet the others at the whirlpool. Her mind was full of the treasure. What would it be? Coins, jewellery, precious gems or gold?

Spotting Kai and Marina just ahead of her with Tommy and Sami, she whizzed up between them. "Isn't this exciting? We're going to find some treas—"

She broke off as they almost swam straight into Glenda Seaglass, a mean mergirl whose father was the Chief of the Guards. For some reason, Glenda had taken against the Save the Sea Creatures Club and was always finding ways to be unkind. She glared at them crossly. "You brainless barnacles! Watch where you're going!"

"Sorry, Glenda!" said Kai.

Glenda sniffed. "You're clumsier than that ugly manatee Luna has as a pet. Where are you going in such a rush anyway?" She frowned. "Did I hear you say something about finding treasure?"

"No!" Coralie exclaimed. She knew if they told Glenda the truth, Glenda would go straight to her dad and then the guards would have all the fun of finding the treasure. Coralie didn't want that at all!

"Definitely not," said Marina, shaking her head hard. "We were just saying we're going to find … find…"

"Find a tremendous amount of rubbish today," Kai invented quickly. "Marina's dad mentioned that there's more litter than usual out on the reef and we thought we'd go and clear it up."

"Litter?" Glenda regarded them suspiciously.

"Yes. We'd better go," said Coralie quickly.

"See you, Glenda!" said Kai as they swam off.

Marina grinned. "Phew! Good thinking there, Kai."

He shook his head. "I'm amazed she believed me."

Coralie wasn't sure Glenda had completely believed them, but at least she hadn't questioned them further. "Come on!" she said, flicking her tail and speeding up. "Naya and Luna will be waiting!"

The five of them gazed at the whirlpool with their pets. "What shall we say?" Naya said as the water foamed and frothed.

"I think Coralie should ask it to take us to the same kelp forest she visited yesterday," said Marina. "Tommy, Dash and Melly, you make sure you dive in with us at the exact same moment. Sami, you and Octavia hold on tight to Naya and me. If you don't, you might end up somewhere completely different!"

Sami curled his tail round a thick strand of Marina's hair and Octavia clung on firmly to Naya's arm.

Coralie saw that Luna was cuddling Melly and looking a little nervous. "Don't worry. It's lovely in the kelp forest, I promise. Ready, everyone?"

They nodded eagerly. "Here goes! Whirlpool, please take us all to the same part of the kelp forest I went to yesterday," Coralie asked.

The waters started to swirl faster. "After three!" she cried. "One … two … THREE!"

She dived in. There was the same whirl of colours as the day before and, after spinning round madly in a rainbow blur, she shot out into the kelp forest. It was even lovelier than she remembered. Long, ribbon-like fronds of kelp were waving in the gentle currents and small fish nibbled at them. The deep greeny-blue water had shafts of sunlight shining through.

The others appeared beside her.

"Wow," said Luna, her eyes wide, as two large orange garibaldi fish swam slowly past them, their mouths opening and closing. "It feels so peaceful here."

"It's quite cold though!" said Naya, shivering.

"It's just like the kelp forest I once went to with my dad," said Marina. "We must be fairly near land as kelp grows in shallow water, normally close to coastlines. We should keep an eye out, just in case there are humans nearby."

"Look at all those sea urchins," said Kai, pointing to a nearby bed of the spiny creatures. "We'd better watch our tails near their spikes!"

Naya picked some old kelp fronds off the rocks and put them in her bag. "I'm going to take these home with me and try experimenting with them. Just look at the way the kelp sticks to the rocks and grows up towards the surface. It's fascinating."

Coralie grinned. "Hey, Marina, what does the seaweed shout when it's stuck at the bottom of the sea?"

"What?" said Marina.

"*Kelp! Kelp!*" said Coralie, swimming away before Marina could throw something at her. Dash clicked his tongue as if he was laughing – at least he always liked her jokes!

Luna squealed in delight as two dark brown sea lions came gliding through the water, using their front flippers to steer their way round the kelp trunks. But Octavia hid behind Naya – sea lions had been known to eat octopus!

One of the sea lions was much smaller than the other and had pale beige rings around his eyes. He swam over to Coralie and Dash and barked at them.

"What's he doing?" asked Kai, surprised.

Coralie grinned. "It's OK," she said, tickling him under the chin as he rubbed his head against her. "Dash and I met this sea lion pup yesterday."

"He's gorgeous," said Luna, holding out a hand and humming softly. The baby sea lion swam straight over to her.

His mother was just as friendly. She nuzzled Luna and Coralie while the others stroked her and her baby.

After a while, the mother and pup began

to play chase, twisting and turning through
the water. Dash and Tommy eagerly joined
in while Coralie and the others watched,
entranced. It was lovely to see the sea lions
playing in their natural environment, free
and happy.

Finally, the mother barked goodbye as she and her pup disappeared up to the surface.

"They can't stay underwater like we can," Marina said. "They're mammals and they have to go to the surface to breathe air every fifteen minutes or so."

Dash whistled and Melly clicked.

"Yes, just like you two!" said Coralie. "Do you want to go with them?"

Dash and Melly nodded and set off.

Coralie took the treasure map out of her bag and unfolded it. "OK. The clue says we need to go past where otters feed. I bet that means we need to go that way." She pointed. "Yesterday I saw an otter diving down to get a sea urchin from that bed over there."

"Should we go to the surface and have a look around?" said Marina.

They nodded and swam upwards, joining Dash and Melly. Cautiously breaking through the surface, they glanced at their surroundings.

To their relief, there was no sign of any humans. Merpeople had to keep hidden from humans at all times.

What they could see was a long, shingle beach with grey stone cliffs rearing up behind it. On one side, very close to them, was a rocky strip of land that jutted out into the sea. Otters were gambolling across it and diving from the rocks into the water. Every so often, one would swim back to the surface with a purple sea urchin in its paws, then it would turn over, float on its back and balance the urchin on its tummy to eat it. On the far side of the bay, there was a similar rocky headland. Coralie could see some animals moving on it, but it was too far away for her to work out what they were. Seals, maybe?

She looked at the playful otters. "I was right. This must be the clue the map talks about – the place where otters feed. So we go past this and then the next instruction says, *seek a rock with a hole.*"

Marina grinned. "What are we waiting for? Let's get seeking!"

"Wait! The trouble is we don't know which way we need to go past the otters," Naya pointed out. "Do we go towards that bit of land over there –" she indicated the rocky strip on the far side of the bay – "or there?" She pointed in the opposite direction from the otters. "Or even out to sea?"

"Maybe we should split up?" Kai suggested. "We'll be able to search a larger area and we should be safe as long as we stay in the kelp forest."

"That's a good plan! Let's all go and explore and meet back here," said Marina.

Coralie saw that Luna was looking nervous.

"Do you and Melly want to come with me and Dash, Luna?" she asked.

"Yes, please," said Luna gratefully.

Promising to meet back there in twenty minutes, they all set off. Coralie and Luna swam across the bay towards the far strip of land. They dived down to search along the bottom, weaving through the trees. They passed rocks of all different shapes and sizes – smooth, jagged and tall – but none that were round with a hole in the middle.

Suddenly Dash gave an alarmed whistle and Melly squeaked, her small eyes widening.

Coralie turned to see two sleek grey-and-white shapes with pointed snouts and tiny black eyes heading towards them through the kelp. One was much smaller than the other, but both moved with a stealthy purpose as they weaved through the seaweed. It was a mother and baby shark!

"Luna! Quick!" she hissed in alarm.

She grabbed her cousin and pulled her
behind an enormous, seaweed-covered boulder.
Dash and Melly hid beside them.

Coralie's heart pounded as she watched the
two sharks swim nearer. The mother didn't
look very big and she had a dark grey body
with a white tummy. Coralie remembered that
Marina had told them that most sharks weren't
dangerous. According to her, the only really
dangerous species were great white sharks
and the occasional bad-tempered reef shark.
But Coralie didn't know what type these two
sharks were. She wished she had concentrated
more in her lessons at school!

Luna moved as if she was about to swim out from behind the boulder. "No!" Coralie hissed, grabbing her hand and holding her fast. Her younger cousin might have a real knack with sea creatures, but there was no way Coralie was going to let her try to make friends with a shark!

The mother shark's head swung towards them. She'd heard Coralie's voice. Leaving her baby, she swam suspiciously towards their hiding place.

Coralie froze in horror. Now what were they going to do?

Chapter Four
Hunting for Treasure

Coralie gripped Luna's hand as the mother shark swam round the rock and stared at them with fierce black eyes.

There was a long pause when no one moved, but, to Coralie's intense relief, the shark simply turned away, swam back to her baby and the pair carried on.

"Oh, Coralie, aren't they sweet?" breathed Luna, pulling herself free and swimming out to watch them leave.

Coralie blinked. The sharks were beautiful

in a sleek, streamlined way, and it had been thrilling to see them so close, but she definitely wouldn't describe them as sweet. "I'm not sure about that," she said, joining Luna. "For a moment, I thought we were going to be shark snacks!" She ran a hand through her wavy hair. "I'm sorry, Luna. I didn't realize there were dangerous things in this forest. Maybe you should have stayed at home on the reef."

"No way! I'm fine. Those sharks weren't dangerous," said Luna. "The mother looked like she just wanted to protect her baby and was checking we weren't a threat. I bet she was travelling through the kelp so she could avoid predators like killer whales. A forest like this must provide her and her baby with perfect protection from bigger, more dangerous creatures."

Coralie nodded. "You're right. She was just looking after her baby, but it was a bit scary. Should we go back and find the others?"

She looked round to see Dash nosing at the seaweed on the boulder. He pulled some off with his teeth. "Come on, Dash!" Coralie called. "Time to get moving!"

He shook his head.

"Dash, what are you doing?" she said.

Dash backed away from the rock and then swam straight at it with an excited look in his eyes.

"Dash! Don't do that—" Coralie broke off with a gasp as Dash hit the centre of the rock and sailed through! It wasn't solid! There was a massive hole in the middle of it that had been covered by the strands of thick seaweed. Dash stopped beside her with seaweed hanging over his face like a wig. He opened his mouth as if he was grinning.

"You've found the round rock with a hole!" Coralie cried, hugging him. "Oh, you clever, clever boy!"

"Oh my goodness!" said Luna, peering

at the rock with Melly. "We have to tell the others about this – it's the first clue!"

Dash whistled at Coralie. She understood.

"Why don't you go and get them, Dash, and we'll stay here? You're so fast, it'll be quicker if you travel on your own. Hurry!"

Dash set off like a silver arrow through the water.

The two mergirls and Melly started to pull the rest of the seaweed off the rock. It looked just like the drawing on the map.

"Where do we have to go next?" Luna said.

Coralie took out the map and read the clue aloud.

"*Treasure in the kelp,*
beyond where otters feed,
Seek a rock with a hole,
head east into the trees,
Past a galaxy of stars
then on to sea lion rock,
Underneath the rookery,
X marks the spot."

She looked up. "From here we need to head east into the forest."

"Let's go to the surface and work out which way east is," said Luna. "We'll be able to tell by looking at the sun."

They swam up and poked their heads through the water. They were very near to the second rocky strip of land now and Coralie could see that the animals she had spotted moving around earlier were mother sea lions and their babies. The other adult sea lions in the colony were sunning themselves on the rocks of the main beach along with a number of grey harbour seals.

"Sea lion mums and pups," breathed Luna. "Can we go and see them?"

"I'd love to but we'd better wait here for now," said Coralie reluctantly. "The others might arrive at any moment with Dash." She looked at the sun. "East is in the direction of the pups though. Maybe we can stop and say hello to them after we've found the treasure."

They dived back down, just in time to see Dash returning with everyone else.

"Over here!" called Coralie, waving.

"You're OK. Phew!" said Marina in relief. "When Dash came to get us and he was on his own, we thought you might be in trouble."

"No, we're fine and look. Ta-da!" Coralie pointed at the rock with a hole in. "We've found the first place on the map!"

The others crowded round and Coralie explained how Dash had found it.

Tommy clapped his flippers, Sami kissed Dash's nose and Octavia patted Dash on the back with her arms.

Dash looked very pleased with himself.

"Now we need to head east," said Marina.

"To a galaxy of stars," said Kai. He frowned. "Do you think that means we need to go to the surface and look at the sky?"

"But we'll only be able to see stars if it's night time," Coralie said. "Are we going to have to come back when it's dark?"

Naya giggled. "Do you two seriously never listen at school? The name for a group of starfish is a galaxy. Don't you remember Sylvie telling us that the other day? I reckon what the clue means is that we need to find a big group of starfish, not look up at the sky!"

Kai grinned at her. "Why would we need to listen when we have you?"

"You know everything," Coralie agreed.

They swam eastwards a little way and found a large group of giant sunflower starfish spread out across the rocks on the seabed. They were each roughly a metre across and had pink-and-purple tentacles.

51

"This must be the galaxy of stars, which means we're almost there!" said Marina excitedly. "We just need to find sea lion rock then a rookery and we'll reach the treasure."

"A rookery?" said Luna. "Isn't that where rooks nest? But rooks are inland birds."

"I think other birds can nest in rookeries too," said Naya. "Maybe it means where some seagulls are nesting."

"We can worry about that later. First we need to find sea lion rock. Look out for a rock shaped like a sea lion, everyone!" Marina said.

They swam and swam, but no matter how hard they looked they couldn't find a sea lion-shaped rock anywhere. In the end they stopped and had their lunch.

"We're going to have to come back another day," said Naya. "We can't stay out much longer. Our parents might get worried and start looking for us. If they realize we've been in the whirlpool, we'll be in trouble."

"But we've got school tomorrow," Kai protested.

"We'll just have to wait until next weekend," said Marina. "If we come here early on Saturday, we can bring a picnic again and spend the whole day searching."

The others nodded.

"We'll find the hidden treasure!" Coralie declared and Dash whistled in agreement. "There's no way we're giving up now!"

Chapter Five
Passing Notes

"I can't stop thinking about the treasure," Marina said to Coralie as they waited to go into school the next morning after saying goodbye to Dash and Sami. Pets were not allowed inside the school, much to the animals' dismay.

Coralie got the map out of her satchel. "Me too. I've been looking at the map, trying to see if there are any more clues…"

"What are you two talking about?" a sharp voice demanded. Glenda Seaglass was right behind them. "Clues to what?" Her eyes narrowed suspiciously as she looked at the rolled-up paper in Coralie's hand. "What's that you've got there, Coralie?"

"Nothing," said Coralie, shoving the map back in her satchel and wondering how much Glenda had overheard.

Glenda's eyes narrowed even more. "You're up to something. Has it got anything to do with your dumb Save the Sea Creatures Club?" She rolled her eyes. "You're such babies! You and your silly pets."

"Go away, Glenda," said Marina. "We don't care what you think, and what we're doing is none of your business."

Coralie groaned inwardly. Marina was great at standing up to Glenda, who could be a real bully, but telling Glenda that something was nothing to do with her was like waving a fish in front of a shark's nose. Coralie had a feeling she'd be even more determined to find out what they were up to now.

To Coralie's relief, the school gong sounded, which meant it was time for lessons to start. "Come on, Marina!" said Coralie, pulling her inside. "Let's go!"

At school, they learned all about oceans so that when they were older they would be able to help look after sea creatures and the underwater environment. They had lessons about sea creatures, natural disasters, human behaviour, mer-myths and mer-magic. The first lesson that morning was on natural disasters. They took notes, using special squid ink that would write underwater, as their teacher – a strict, dark-haired mermaid called Sylvie – taught them about storms.

Coralie didn't like school much. She found sitting still and listening quite difficult. She much preferred to be out swimming on the coral reef, and Kai was the same. While Naya, Marina and Luna carefully wrote down what the teacher was saying with their seagull-quill pens, Coralie passed a note to Kai.

I wish we were in the forest!

He scribbled a reply underneath.

Me too. I hope we find the SL rock on Saturday!

He passed the note back. Coralie started to add another line.

Yeah! Can you imagine everyone's faces if we come back with a load of—

"Miss! Miss!" Glenda's hand shot up. "Coralie and Kai are passing notes to each other!"

Coralie froze as Sylvie swam over and plucked the note from Coralie's hands.

"Coralie! Kai! This is not the kind of behaviour I expect from you two. You can both do an extra sheet of questions for me for wasting time in class. Now get on with your work."

"Sorry, Miss," said Coralie and Kai.

Sylvie tossed the note in the bin and continued to talk about the damage storms could do to underwater environments. Glenda gave Coralie a smug look and Coralie pulled a face at her. Glenda was as mean as a reef shark with toothache!

For the rest of the lesson, Coralie worked hard and took notes like everyone else. She didn't want to get into any more trouble. It was a relief when breaktime came and she could put her quill down. "At last," she muttered to Kai. "I need a swim!"

"Miss, would you like me to tidy up the classroom during break?" Glenda asked, giving Sylvie the wide-eyed, *I'm-such-a-perfect-mergirl* look that she kept especially for teachers and other adults.

"Thank you, Glenda, that's very kind of you," said Sylvie. "You can have an extra seashell point for offering to help."

Glenda smiled sweetly. "Thank you, Miss."

Coralie and her friends swam out of the classroom. "What's Glenda up to?" Marina said. "She never offers to help tidy up. She's usually as lazy as a sea slug!"

"I don't know and I don't care," said Coralie.

"I can't believe she told Sylvie you were writing notes," said Luna. "That was so mean."

"And now we've got extra homework," sighed Kai.

"At least Sylvie didn't make you stay late after school," said Naya. "Does everyone want to go litter picking on the reef when classes are finished?"

They nodded. Although the reef was far away from any humans, plastic often still reached them on the ocean currents and it could cause a lot of damage to the coral, and great harm to sea creatures, so they always tried to collect any litter. Their reef stretched for miles beyond the merpeople's caves and they often went swimming on it after school, collecting litter as they travelled.

"I've got something I want to try while we're there," said Naya.

"A new invention?" asked Luna eagerly.

"More of a science experiment really," Naya replied. "Kelp is supposed to be a good fertilizer – it helps plants grow – so I tried mixing the kelp fronds with some of my mum's mermaid powder. I'm hoping I've made a kind of growing potion. I really want to try it out on a patch of seagrass and see what happens."

Glenda came swimming up, waving a piece of paper and looking triumphant. "I knew it!" she exclaimed. "I knew you losers were up to something!"

Coralie's heart sank. Glenda was holding the note that she and Kai had been writing to each other in class. She must have asked if she could tidy up just so she could take it out of the bin. They should have guessed.

"What are you talking about?" Marina said, frowning. "Sometimes you make no more sense than a babble fish, Glenda."

"Oh really?" Glenda read out the words on the paper. *"I wish we were in the forest… I hope we find the SL rock on Saturday… Can you imagine everyone's faces if we come back with…"* Her eyes narrowed. "What forest? What are you doing on Saturday?"

"It's nothing to do with you." Coralie glared back at her.

"I'll tell my dad if you don't let me know what's going on," threatened Glenda.

"Tell him," said Marina, shrugging. "What's

he going to do? We're not doing anything wrong."

"Yeah, we're just playing a game," said Kai quickly.

"Come on, everyone." Marina started to swim away. "Let's play tag!"

The others swam after her.

"Sorry," Coralie whispered to them. "We shouldn't have written that note."

"It's no big deal," Marina reassured her. "The note didn't give much away. Glenda doesn't know anything important. I bet she'll forget about it soon."

Coralie glanced back at Glenda. She wasn't so sure. The blond mergirl was watching them with her hands on her hips and a determined look in her eyes.

Chapter Six
Glenda the Spy

After school, Dash whooshed up to Coralie, butted her affectionately with his head, then raced round her in excited circles and sped off.

Coralie charged after him. "I'm so glad school's finished. My tail is cramped from sitting still."

"Let's go and pick up some litter on the reef and save some sea creatures!" said Kai, grabbing Tommy's shell and letting the turtle pull him along.

"Then I can try out my potion and we can

check to see if any sea dragons have hatched yet," added Naya. A few weeks ago, she had made some nesting boxes to protect the sea dragons – little creatures that were the size of a seahorse but looked like tiny dragons – as they hatched their eggs.

"I'll need to ask Mum if I can come with you," said Luna. She wasn't allowed to go out on to the reef after school, like the older ones were, without asking permission. "Can we stop at the Marine Sanctuary on the way?"

"Of course," Marina replied.

The sanctuary was very near school. As Luna swam in to find her mum, the others clustered together and told the pets about Glenda reading the note.

"Luckily it didn't say anything about fin—" Coralie broke off as Dash whistled a warning and waved his flipper. Glancing over her shoulder, she saw Glenda had followed them and was listening in.

Coralie hastily lowered her voice to a whisper. "About you-know-what!" she hissed.

Luna came swimming back to them with her mum, Erin.

"Hi there!" Erin said. "It's fine for Luna to come with you and check on the sea dragons and, while you're near the meadow, can you do something for me? There's a cave beside it where a group of giant cuttlefish have gathered and I'm hoping they're going to lay their eggs in there. Could you check to see if there are any? You'll have to be very quiet so you don't startle them."

"No problem! We'd love to have a look at them for you, Auntie Erin, and we'll make sure to be quiet," said Coralie. Cuttlefish were related to octopus and squid and they shot out clouds of black ink whenever they felt threatened.

"Thank you! You'll be able to spot the cave – it's completely covered in barnacles. Have fun and see you later," Erin said.

"OK, and Auntie Erin…" said Coralie.

"Oh no, I know that tone of voice. It's another joke," groaned Naya. "Quick, everyone! Swim!"

"What did the baby cuttlefish say to its mum when it hurt itself?" Coralie asked her aunt.

Erin raised her eyebrows. "I don't know. What did it say, Coralie?"

"Please can I have a *cuttle*?" Coralie said. She swam off after the others, laughing to herself as her aunt rolled her eyes and suppressed a smile.

It was lovely to be out on the reef after a day at school. It stretched on and on through the ocean. Clouds of fish streamed by and pale anemones waved their tentacles from the banks of multicoloured coral as crabs, lobsters and starfish edged across the sand and rocks.

As Coralie and the others swam to the seagrass meadow, they gathered up any rubbish they saw – bottles and straws, plastic bags and bits of broken netting. They put them in their satchels so that sea creatures didn't get tangled up in the plastic or try to eat it.

Every so often, Dash glanced round sharply. "What is it?" Coralie asked, not seeing anything unusual behind them. Dash whistled but she didn't understand.

Finally they reached the large seagrass meadow. They headed to the barnacle-covered cave that Luna's mum had told them about. Peeping in, they saw eight giant cuttlefish resting on the bottom of the cave. The cuttlefish were about fifty centimetres long, their bodies covered in bright orange-and-blue patterns.

"No eggs yet," whispered Coralie, keeping her voice down so she didn't startle them.

"Let's leave them in peace," whispered Naya. "I don't want to get covered in ink."

"Definitely not – it takes days to wear off,"
whispered Kai. "I sat on a cuttlefish once. It
squirted me and I was grey for a week!"

They left the cave and swam into the
meadow. It was a large flat area of seagrass
where turtles and manatees grazed. Tommy
and Melly swam off to say hello while the
others checked the nesting boxes. They were
buried among the seagrass. The idea was that
the babies could hatch safely, away from hungry
fish, and when they left the nesting boxes
they'd be able to live happily in the meadow,
feeding on the plankton there.

Coralie and the others checked each nesting
box, lifting the lids and peering inside. Sami
looked in too. It was the male sea dragons that
looked after the eggs, not the females – just like
with seahorses. In every nesting box there was
a father with a fat pouch of eggs but no babies
yet. Coralie smiled. Hopefully there would be
loads of babies soon!

As Coralie shut the lid of one, Dash spun round in alarm.

"You're being really jumpy today," said Coralie, following his gaze to a large group of tall sea sponges at one side of meadow. She stroked him. "What's up? There's nothing there."

Naya swam over. "No babies yet but hopefully it won't be long! Now I'm going to try out my growing potion," she announced after she'd finished examining the nesting boxes. "I'll put some on the grass over by those sponges and monitor it when we come back here to check on the sea dragons. I'll be able to see if it grows more than the surrounding grass and, if it does, I'll know my potion works. I can't wait to see what happens!" She swam over to the sponges and uncorked the bottle. She scattered a few drops on to the seagrass and then swam back to the others. Just as she reached them, there was a green flash.

"Jumping jellyfish!" exclaimed Marina as the grass where Naya had scattered the potion suddenly shot up by about three metres.

Naya gasped and Luna giggled. "I think your potion works, Naya!"

"A bit too well!" Kai said with a grin.

There was a shriek and the grass started to move from side to side as if something was trying to fight its way out from inside.

"Something's in there," said Naya in alarm.

"Not something but someone!" exclaimed Coralie as Glenda fought her way out of the gigantic grasses. The blond mergirl had stalks caught in her hair, scratches on her arms and face, and she was furious.

"Look at the state of me!" she screamed at them.

"What were you doing in there?" said Marina, astonished.

"I… I…" Glenda spluttered.

"She was spying on us!" Coralie realized. "Dash kept hearing something behind us. It must have been Glenda following us."

"As if I'd waste my time following you boring barnacles!" Glenda spat. "Of course I wasn't spying on you. I was… I was just out for a swim."

"So why were you hiding behind the sea sponges?" said Naya.

Glenda glared at them. "I wasn't! I… I… Oh, I've had enough of this. I'm going!" she exclaimed angrily and swam away.

"She was definitely spying on us," said Kai.

Coralie grinned. "Well, hopefully she's learned her lesson and she'll stay away from us from now on!"

However, the encounter seemed to make Glenda even more determined to find out what the others were up to. Every time they tried to chat, they found Glenda listening in and, each day after school, she followed them as they swam out on the reef.

"Why won't she leave us alone?" groaned Coralie on Friday night. They had gone to her cave after school – somewhere Glenda couldn't follow. All five of them and their pets were packed tightly into her small bedroom so they could talk in peace.

"Do you think she knows we're looking for treasure," said Marina, "and she doesn't want us to be the ones who find it?"

"She was really cross when we solved the mystery of how the deep reef was being damaged," said Naya. "I bet she won't want us doing anything like that again."

"It's lucky she doesn't realize that the treasure isn't actually here," said Kai. "She can follow us all over the reef if she likes and it won't do her any good."

"But what are we going to do if she follows us to the whirlpool tomorrow morning?" Luna pointed out.

There was a silence and then Coralie started to giggle. "You know, I think I might have an idea!"

Chapter Seven
Back to the Floating Forest

After some intense planning, everyone left Coralie's cave to go home. They milled around the entrance, talking loudly.

"See you on the reef tomorrow then, Coralie!" Kai said clearly.

"We'll meet after lunch by the sea meadow," said Marina. "That's the sea meadow, everyone. Have you got that?"

"Yes," they chorused.

"And you've got the treasure map, haven't you, Naya?" Coralie called.

"Yes, it's here," said Naya, patting a rolled-up piece of paper that was sticking out of the top of her satchel. "I'll make sure I keep it very safe." She winked at the others. "See you all tomorrow afternoon." They waved and headed off to their homes.

Peeping out from her cave, Coralie saw Naya shift the bag on her shoulder, dislodging the rolled-up paper that was sticking out, just as they'd planned. It wasn't the real treasure map, but one Naya had drawn, showing the reef and the sea meadow. As the fake map fell out of her bag, Naya pretended not to notice and carried on her way.

A few minutes later, Coralie saw Glenda look out from behind a giant clamshell.

Checking to see that there was no one watching, the blond mermaid swam over to the fake map and picked it up.

"I think this is going to work!" Coralie whispered gleefully to Dash. He whistled as Glenda stuffed the piece of paper into her satchel and quickly swam away.

After a very early breakfast the next morning, Coralie raced to meet the others by Mermaids Rock. Most merpeople were still in their caves. The sun was only just coming up and the early-morning water was cool. The reef always felt different first thing – quieter and stiller. The fish swam slowly when the water was colder. They drifted about, feeding on plankton and nibbling gently at the coral. Crabs came creeping out from their holes and turtles emerged from under the coral ledges where they slept at night. Coralie marvelled at the peaceful world around her and was relieved to see there was no sign of Glenda – it looked like their plan had worked!

Naya and Luna were already at the whirlpool and Marina and Kai joined them a few minutes later.

"Is everyone ready?" said Marina. "Have you got the map, Coralie – the real one?"

"Yes, it's here! Has everyone told their parents they'll be out all day so they don't come looking for us?" Coralie asked.

The friends nodded.

"I've got a bag to collect more kelp," said Naya. "I'm developing a growing potion that works properly, rather than making things much taller in two seconds! And I've got one of these for everybody." She showed them jars that had a small bag of liquid sitting on top of a silvery powder. "It's a new invention of mine."

"What are they?" said Kai, looking at his curiously. He started to shake it.

"Don't do that!" Naya said quickly. "They're emergency lights. If you shake them hard, then the little bag will burst. When the liquid spills on to the mermaid powder, the two things react and start glowing. I got the idea from the bioluminescent fish we saw when we were on the deep reef – the ones that glow in the dark. I collected some bioluminescent algae from there to make the liquid. The lights will only work once, and they'll last for about half an hour, so don't use them unless you have to."

"Awesome!" said Marina enthusiastically.

Coralie nodded. "It's a *krill-iant* invention. It'll be just what we need if the treasure is hidden somewhere dark." Her eyes sparkled. "We're going to find the treasure today even if we have to search the whole forest!" She swam closer to the whirlpool. "Take us to the kelp forest we went to last Sunday," she asked it. "To the exact same place, please."

The water started to whirl and swirl.

"Come on, Dash!" Coralie cried and they dived in together. Just as before, the water swirled round them like a wild rainbow. Coralie spun round and round and then she shot out.

She blinked her eyes open, expecting to see the beautiful, serene forest with seals and sea lions swimming through the bluey-green water, but, to her surprise, everywhere looked completely different. The water was a dark, murky colour filled with sand and fronds. The kelp trees had been torn from the rocky bottom and were floating at the surface of the water in a thick layer, blocking out the light. The occasional sad-looking fish swam past, the sea urchins on the bottom had kelp fronds caught on their spines and there were no otters, seals or sea lions to be seen anywhere.

Coralie heard the others' startled exclamations as they arrived.

"What's happened?" Kai said.

"Where are all the animals?" asked Luna.

"It must have been a storm like Sylvie told us about at school" said Naya, pushing a bunch of kelp away from her face.

"It's destroyed the whole forest," said Coralie in dismay.

"Do you think the creatures are hurt?" said Luna. Melly rubbed her head reassuringly against Luna's arm.

"I think they'll be OK," said Marina quickly. "The seals, sea lions and otters would have sheltered on land during the storm and any of the creatures that couldn't go onshore would have swum away deep into the ocean before the kelp was ripped up." She shook her head. "It was such a beautiful forest that protected so many animals, and now it's destroyed. This is awful!"

The others nodded. The treasure suddenly didn't seem important at all.

"Can we do anything to help repair it?" said Coralie.

"Clearing the kelp from the surface would be a good idea," said Naya. "If we push the torn trees on to the land, then that will let sunlight into the water, which will help new kelp start to grow."

They swam up to the surface. The kelp was floating there like a thick green-and-brown carpet. A little way off was the rocky strip of land where the otters lived. They were picking their way forlornly across the seaweed-covered rocks, staring at the water as if wondering whether to try to dive down to find a sea urchin to eat.

"At least the otters look OK," said Coralie in relief. She frowned suddenly as she spotted an otter that looked bigger than the others. It was right at the end of the spit of land and had a longer neck and pale patches around its eyes. It opened its mouth and barked sadly.

Coralie gasped. "Look!" she exclaimed. "It's the sea lion pup we met. What's he doing over there with the otters?"

"Maybe he got separated from his mother in the storm and was swept on to the rocks," said Naya anxiously. "Oh, the poor thing!"

"This looks like a job for the Save the Sea Creatures Club," said Kai.

"Should we bring him back to the reef and take him to the sanctuary?" Coralie said.

"No," Marina said quickly. "Our warm reef isn't the right habitat for him. He needs to stay here." She glanced around. "We can help him though. Let's take him to where the sea lion babies and mothers are and then we can try to

86

find his mother."

"He sounds so sad," said Luna as the sea lion barked mournfully again.

"Sea lions hate being on their own," said Naya. "They're used to being part of a big group. It must be really scary for him to be away from his mother and his friends."

Luna started heading towards him, pushing the seaweed out of the way. "Ugh! It's so hard to swim through this kelp!"

"Keep pushing it towards the land," advised Naya. "The more we can clear it off the surface, the better."

Their pets joined them, pushing the kelp towards the rocks with their snouts, flippers and arms. Only Sami was too small to help. He tucked himself into Marina's hair to keep out of the way.

The young sea lion watched them approaching. He had been so friendly and confident before the storm when they'd seen him with his mum, but now he shrank back and made a trumpeting sound, his eyes wide and fearful. The storm had made him nervous.

"Don't be scared," said Luna. "We're here to help." She started to hum. The sea lion cocked his head to one side, listening. Gradually, the fear faded from his eyes and the tension left his body. The others hung back and let Luna go closer. She swam over to the rocks and pulled herself out, leaving the end of her tail dangling in the water. He flapped his way over to meet her and stretched out his whiskery muzzle.

She gently stroked him and he tried to climb on to her lap. She giggled. "You're heavier than you look!" He thrust his muzzle into her neck, hiding his head under her long red hair. Luna hugged him and looked at her friends. "We have to help him join the other sea lions."

They nodded. There was no question about it.

"We'll do that, then we must do what we can to repair the damage," said Marina.

"And clear the seaweed off the sea urchins," said Naya, seeing an otter pop up through the water with a kelp-covered urchin in its paws.

"But first we help Barney," said Luna. "That's what I'm calling him." She kissed the sea lion. "Come on, Barney. We're going to find your mum!"

She lowered him into the water. Dash and Melly greeted the pup by rubbing noses with him, Tommy and Octavia waved and Sami swam round his head, waggling his horns in a friendly way. Barney looked much happier.

"Let's swim deeper underwater," said Coralie. "It'll be easier than fighting through the kelp up here."

They dived down to the bottom. The water was murky and dim and they had to swim with their arms outstretched so they didn't bump into anything. Barney swam in between Dash and Melly with Naya and Luna on either side, while Marina, Coralie and Sami led the way. Kai and Tommy brought up the rear. Last weekend the kelp forest had seemed like a safe haven, but now it was eerie and full of shadows. Coralie could feel her heart beating faster than normal.

"It's very dark… Should we use the lights you made, Naya?" she said uneasily.

"Remember they can only be used once," Naya reminded her. "Let's try to swim without them, but if it gets much darker then yes, we probably should."

A large black fish, almost as big as Dash, swam out in front of them. Coralie and Marina stopped so abruptly that the others almost swam into them.

"It's just a bass," said Marina, relieved. Black bass were big but very gentle. "Let's keep going."

They swam on until something long and thin slithered in front of their noses. Once again, they stopped with a start, but it was just a harmless moray eel. Coralie told herself to stop being so jumpy. It was hard though.

Without the protection of the kelp trees, the water felt dangerous and unsafe. *That's because it* is *dangerous*

and unsafe, she thought. Before the storm, the kelp forest had stopped any large predators like killer whales or great white sharks from coming too close to the shore. However, without the trees, there was no shelter for them or any of the animals.

Dash whistled at her and motioned upwards with his snout.

"Dash needs to get some air," Coralie said.

"Barney should get some too," said Luna.

"We can swim up to see how near we are to the sea lion colony," said Marina.

They nodded and headed towards the surface. Dash broke through the kelp and arched over the sea, blowing a fountain of water out from his blowhole. Barney stuck his head out and took a gulp of air. Shaking the kelp from her hair, Coralie looked towards the rocks where the mother and baby sea lions were gathered. They were close enough to hear their barks and calls. Barney barked excitedly in response.

Luna smiled. "Yes, Barney. We'll have you back with your friends very soon. You're going to be fine."

"Oh no, no, no, no, no!" Marina gasped suddenly.

Hearing the fear in her voice, Coralie swung round. "What is it?" She didn't think she'd ever heard Marina sound scared before.

Marina's face was pale as she pointed across the waves to where three huge whales were swimming towards the land. Their backs and fins were a shiny black and their bellies were white. "Killer whales!" she exclaimed.

Chapter Eight
Attack!

Icy fear ran down Coralie's spine as she stared at the huge black-and-white whales heading straight towards them. Killer whales – orcas – were vicious creatures with sharp teeth who loved to hunt their prey down through the water. They would eat anything – seals, sea lions, manatees, turtles, dolphins and definitely mer-people. They were some of the most dangerous creatures in the ocean and you really didn't want to be in the water with them!

"What are we going to do?" cried Naya.

Dash, Melly, Tommy, Sami and Octavia swam in terrified circles. On the rocky coastline the mother sea lions had spotted the approaching whales too. Their friendly barking changed to alarmed trumpeting and they started shepherding their babies away from the edges of the headland where the whales could snap them up. The ones closest to the cliffs and the beach started pushing the babies on to the land and up the cliffs as far from the sea as possible. The other adult sea lions and seals also hastily wriggled their way further up the rocks to get away. Panicked roars and barks filled the air.

"I'm scared!" cried Luna.

"What should we do?" Coralie yelled to Marina.

"I don't know!" For once, Marina looked completely out of ideas.

Barney started to bark over and over again.

He dived beneath the water and then poked his head back up and barked again. He did that several times.

"What's he doing?" shouted Kai.

"I've no idea." Coralie noticed that the sea lion mothers who were near the end of the headland and far away from the cliffs were now pushing their babies into the water and diving in after them. "What are they doing?" she said, pointing. "Why are they getting into the water?"

"They're going to be eaten if they do that!" shrieked Luna as the orcas arched over the waves, showing off their gleaming white bellies. As they splashed back into the water, Coralie felt the impact in the sea around her.

Grabbing Luna's hand gently in his mouth, Barney tried to tug her downwards.

"What are you doing, Barney?" Luna exclaimed. She looked into his eyes for a moment, then her voice changed. "Everyone, I think Barney is trying to tell me something. I think he wants us to go under the water with him."

"Maybe there's a safe place somewhere down there!" gasped Marina. "That must be why the mother sea lions who can't reach the cliffs in time are taking their babies into the water. Follow Barney, everyone!"

Luna dived down with the sea lion and the others followed her.

They swam deeper and deeper, the headland looming in front of them like a cliff face. Peering through the gloomy water, Coralie realized where Barney was heading – there was a wide crack in the base of the headland that was protected by overhanging rocks. It looked like the entrance to an underwater cave. The mother sea lions were pushing

their babies through the crack with their noses and following them in. The last sea lion disappeared inside and Barney followed. Glancing round, Coralie saw the large black-and-white head of one of the orcas appearing through the murkiness. Its eyes gleamed viciously as it saw them and its gigantic mouth opened, revealing sharp teeth.

"Quick!" Coralie shrieked as her friends and their pets dived through the crack. Coralie was last.

The orca's jaws snapped shut, just missing her tail fin by centimetres. Her heart almost jumped out of her chest as she heard the clashing of its teeth, but she was safe! The orca hadn't touched her and it was far too big to follow them inside.

Where were they? She peered around but it was pitch-black and impossible to see anything. The water buzzed with the sound of the mothers barking and the pups whimpering. Coralie could feel the sea lions' bodies jostling around her in the water.

"I can't see anything," she heard Marina say.

"There seems to be some light over this way," she heard Kai call above the sea lions.

"I'll use my emergency light," said Naya. "But we should keep the rest of yours safe. We don't know how long we're going to be down here." There was the sound of her rummaging in her satchel and then the noise of something being shaken.

Bright green light blazed out. Naya held up the jar and Coralie realized that they were in a tunnel, not a cave. It was packed with sea lions queuing to get through an opening at the end, from which the faint light was glowing. Barney barked and beckoned to them with his head.

"He wants us to go with them," said Luna.

Naya led the way with her light, following the sea lions. Swimming through the opening, they gasped. Now they were in an underwater cave – an enormous one! It was completely filled with water and its roof was covered with glowing plankton that cast a gentle green light.

The mother sea lions swam about, reunited with their babies. They were nuzzling them and patting them with their flippers, but Coralie hardly noticed. Her attention was caught by an enormous treasure chest on the floor of the cave... The wood was old and rotten, but golden jewellery and precious gems spilled out of it. As she watched, a pair of sea lion pups picked up a gold necklace and started playing tug of war with it. Other pups tossed glittering jewels to each other like balls, cleverly catching them on their noses before throwing them back.

"The treasure!" breathed Marina.

"We've actually found it!" exclaimed Kai.

"And look at how much the sea lions love playing with it," said Luna in delight as one of the pups balanced a ring on the end of its nose while another two started batting a large ruby between them with their flippers. The mother sea lions watched happily as their pups frolicked in the treasure. "It looks like they come here a lot. It's their playground!"

"Of course!" Coralie exclaimed, hitting her forehead. "Now I get what the clue on the map meant! I can't believe I didn't realize before." Seeing her friends' confused expressions, she quoted it to them.

"Past a galaxy of stars
then on to sea lion rock,
Underneath the rookery,
X marks the spot."

She shook her head. "We thought sea lion rock meant a rock that was shaped like a sea lion, but it must have meant the rocky headland where the sea lions live. And rookery is also the name for a group of mother and baby sea lions and where they gather. It was on that sheet of extra questions that Kai and I had to do. The treasure was here, underneath the rookery, the whole time!"

"That clue was nothing to do with rooks or seagulls then?" said Marina.

"No, nothing at all. We got that completely wrong," Coralie replied.

"I should have remembered what a rookery was." Naya grinned at Coralie and Kai. "Maybe *I* need to listen in class more!"

"Or you could just rely on us always getting extra homework," Coralie said, grinning back.

"We've found the treasure!" said Kai.

"This is *fin-tastic!*"

"And that's not all we've found…" said Luna. "Look!" She pointed to where Barney was nuzzling up to a mother sea lion. She was covering his face with kisses and he was cuddling close to her, his eyes shining with happiness. "Barney's found his mum," said Luna as the little sea lion laid his cheek against his mother's.

Coralie gave her a hug. "I'm so pleased. He looks really happy, doesn't he?"

Luna nodded. "He's back where he belongs. Safe and sound." A look of alarm crossed her face. "Wait, but he's not safe, is he? None of the sea lions are. The orcas are still out in the sea and after a while the sea lions are going to have to get some air. What'll happen when they leave the cave? They'll be eaten! Dash and Melly too!"

The friends exchanged worried looks. Luna was right. It would be very dangerous for the sea lions and Dash and Melly to leave the cave while there were hungry orcas around, but they couldn't stay underwater forever.

"What are we going to do?" Luna asked anxiously. "We can't let them be eaten. We just can't!"

Chapter Nine
Saving
the Sea Lions

"Why don't we see if the orcas are still there?" said Marina. "They might have gone."

Using Naya's light, they swam back down the dark tunnel to the crack in the rocks.

"Who's going to have a look out there?" said Coralie, staring at the entrance. "The orcas could be lurking, just waiting for something to appear."

Sami let go of Marina's hair and bobbed towards the opening. He looked at it and back at the rest of them.

"OK, you go, Sami," said Marina. "If there are any orcas, they won't be interested in eating a seahorse. You're much too small. But be careful – they could squash you."

Sami nodded hard and swam out. They waited nervously. A few minutes later, he returned. He looked happy and relieved and motioned with his head that they should follow him.

Swimming cautiously through the opening, they looked around and saw that there was no sign of the killer whales. They must have given up and moved on. Coralie noticed something else too.

"The water's lighter," she pointed out.

Naya looked up. "The orcas are so big they must have pushed a lot of the surface kelp towards the shore as they swam through it. The water is much clearer and the sunlight's getting through again – that will help the kelp grow back."

"How long do you think it'll take the forest to regrow?" Coralie asked Naya.

"Kelp grows quickly, but it'll take a couple of months for it to get back to how it was, and be thick enough to stop the orcas coming so close to the shore," Naya said. "Until then, all the animals here will be in danger."

"Oh, I wish we could make it grow back more quickly!" exclaimed Luna.

Coralie stared at her. "We can! Naya, can't we use your growing potion?"

Naya's eyes widened. "Yes! That's a really *foam-tastic* idea!"

"It is but there's only one bottle," Kai pointed out. "That's not going to be enough to grow a whole forest back, is it?"

Coralie's heart sank. That was true. They'd be able to grow some of the kelp back super-quickly, but not enough to keep the orcas away from the seals, sea lions and otters.

"I can easily make some more," said

Naya, looking round. "All I need is kelp and mermaid powder."

"But we don't have any mermaid powder here," Coralie pointed out.

"Oh, yes we do," said Naya triumphantly, holding up her light. "The lights have got mermaid powder in! I can get the powder out of the jars I made you and that should give me just enough to make the potion I need to regrow the whole forest!"

Marina whooped. "Naya, you're a genius!"

Coralie swam in an excited circle. "Let's get started straight away!"

Naya made her way to the sea lions' headland and pulled herself up on to the rocks. She carefully emptied the mermaid powder from the unused jars on to a dry piece of seaweed and found a sharp stone. While she got everything ready, the others raced around, collecting kelp. The pets helped too, carrying it back in their mouths. Naya used the stone to grind the kelp up, and then scraped the green paste into the jars. She put a large pinch of mermaid powder into each jar, mixed it with the paste and added some seawater. "Done!" she declared at last. She gave the jars to her friends and took the original potion bottle out of her bag. "We're good to go!"

"Let's spread out across the bay," Marina suggested. "That way we'll cover a bigger area. Coralie, you and Dash are the fastest so why don't you swim over to near the otters? Luna, you stay here, by the sea lions, and the rest of us will fill in the gaps between you."

"Sprinkle a few drops on the kelp at the bottom of the ocean, swim quickly out of the way and then repeat!" Naya instructed.

"Until the potion has gone and the trees have regrown," said Coralie happily. "Let's go, Dash!"

They streaked away. By the time they had reached the rocks where the otters gathered, Coralie could already see flashes of light coming from behind them as the potion worked. The kelp grew instantly from small plants on the rocky bed to fully grown trees with canopies of healthy green fronds. It was great fun sprinkling the potion and watching the kelp shoot up to the surface.

"Whoosh!" exclaimed Coralie as a clump of kelp sprang up next to her. She sprinkled a few more drops. "And whoosh again!"

Dash whistled gleefully and turned a somersault.

When Coralie had used up her potion, she swam back to the others.

"We did it! We regrew the forest!" Marina declared as they sat on the rocks at the edge of the rookery and looked at the kelp forest now spreading out across the bay once more. Dash, Octavia and Tommy were playing chase in the water beside them while Melly lay next to Luna on the rocks and Sami bobbed around in the water by Marina's tail fin. Behind them, the mother sea lions and their pups had come out of the treasure cave and were basking in the sun, the pups' muzzles resting on the mothers' backs.

"And now the animals here will be safe from predators again," said Luna.

Coralie sighed happily.

116

It was an amazing feeling to know
that they had been able to help restore
the forest. She couldn't wait until she was
old enough to spend her days travelling
round the world, helping sort out
environmental disasters.

"You're so clever," Coralie said to Naya. "Your inventions completely saved the day."

Naya shrugged. "Pity I wasn't smart enough to remember what a rookery was last weekend! We could have finished the treasure hunt then if I'd remembered." She flashed a smile at Coralie. "Thank goodness you worked it out!"

"But if we'd figured that out last weekend then we wouldn't have been here to help Barney find his mum and help regrow the forest," said Marina. "So it worked out for the best after all."

"What do you think we should do about the treasure?" Kai asked.

For a moment, no one spoke.

"Um…" Coralie didn't want to upset the others but she had to say what she thought. "I actually think we should leave it here." She rushed on before they could speak. "The sea lion pups like playing with the treasure so it should stay put. It's part of their lives and their habitat."

A look of relief crossed her friends' faces.

"I was thinking exactly the same thing!" said Kai.

"Me too," agreed Marina.

"If we take it home, it'll just be put in a museum. I'd rather we left it here for the sea lions," said Luna.

"It can be our secret," said Naya. "No one else needs to know."

"The treasure stays!" Marina declared.

They ate their lunch and watched the sea lions. As the sun started to edge downwards in the sky, the sea lions became more active again, diving into the water and playing games, sticking their heads up and barking at the girls and Kai.

Barney came swimming over and stared at them. "I think he wants us to play with him," said Luna.

They dived into the ocean. Soon they were having races with the sea lion pups, weaving in and out of the kelp, then catching them and having whiskery sea lion kisses and cuddles. Coralie's heart swelled with happiness. Treasure hunting had been good fun, but playing with the sea lions, her friends and their pets was even better!

At last, it was time to make their way back to the reef. They all gave Barney a last stroke. He kissed Luna's nose, then they said goodbye and headed back to the small whirlpool near where the otters lived.

"I wish we didn't have to leave the sea lions," said Luna.

"We'll come back here," said Coralie. "We'll make sure we visit regularly so that if there's another storm we can help repair the forest again."

Luna smiled at her. "Promise?"

"Promise," Coralie replied.

Chapter Ten
Safe and Sound

Their work done, the friends dived into the whirlpool and came out by Mermaids Rock. After being in the cool green waters of the forest for so long, it felt strange being back in the warm, bright water of the coral reef. Shoals of fish were whizzing around and turtles were zooming through the water. Tired but happy, they headed for their homes. On the way they passed the cave where Glenda lived with her mum and dad. There were shrieks coming from inside.

"I can't go to school on Monday looking like this! Everyone will laugh. Do something, Mum!"

Coralie glanced at the others and they swam closer, curiously.

"There, there, sweetie," they heard Glenda's mum say soothingly. "It'll soon fade."

Next they heard Glenda's dad's deep voice. "What I don't understand is why you went into that cave, Glenda. Didn't you see the cuttlefish?"

"Only when I was inside, and then they all shot ink at me before I could get out! I told you – I went in because I thought there was treasure in there."

"But why did you think that?" Chief Razeem said, surprised.

"I just did!" Glenda appeared in the cave entrance. "And now look at me!" she wailed.

Coralie and the others gasped. Glenda's blond hair and pale skin were now a dark grey. Hearing their gasps, she swung round and saw them. "You lot!" she exclaimed, swimming out of the cave and pointing angrily at them. "This is all your fault! It was your stupid map that led me into that cave!"

Her mum and dad followed her out.

"Map?" said Kai innocently.

"Oh, Glenda, you didn't find the map that we'd drawn, did you? It was just a game we were playing. It wasn't a real treasure map, silly!" Marina added.

Glenda shrieked in annoyance and the noise made the nearby merpeople look round. They started to point at Glenda and bite back smiles and chuckles.

"Mummy! Everybody's laughing at me!" Glenda wailed.

"Let's go back inside, sweetie," said her mum, ushering her into the cave.

Chief Razeem gave Coralie and the others a cross look and waved his hand at them.

"Go on, move along! There's nothing to see here."

They swam off. As soon as they were away from the cave, Coralie burst out laughing. "I guess our trick worked then!"

"Better than we ever imagined," said Marina. "I've no idea why Glenda went into the cuttlefish cave. We didn't draw it on the map."

"She must have seen us going there the other day when she was spying on us and thought that might be where the treasure was hidden," said Naya.

"Poor Glenda," said Luna. "She won't like having grey hair for a few days."

"Maybe it will make her *ink* twice about spying on us again though!" said Coralie with a grin and for once everyone laughed.

"It really has been an awesome day!" said Kai. "Regrowing a kelp forest, finding treasure…"

"Escaping from orcas," Marina put in.

"And rescuing Barney," added Luna.

Naya's eyes shone. "You know what, I can't wait for our next adventure!"

"If we work together, we can solve any mystery! The Save the Sea Creatures Club is the best!" said Coralie. She held up her hand and everyone high-fived her.

"The very best!" they all exclaimed.

Turn the page to learn more about stunning kelp forests and the creatures that live there!

KELP FORESTS

Kelp forests are one of the most diverse environments in the ocean. They are home to a wide range of animals, including sea otters, gulls, sea lions, seals, whales and terns. The thick fronds provide shelter from predators, as well as food for hungry creatures!

Kelp needs for light for photosynthesis. This means they are generally found in shallower water, of depths of around 12.5 to 40 metres. When conditions are good, kelp can grow up to 45 centimetres per day.

Big storms can damage kelp forests. This usually happens over winter, and then the forest will start to grow again in the spring.

It's not just sea creatures that use kelp. We use it too! It can be found in everyday products such as shampoo, toothpastes and medicine.

MEET DASH THE DOLPHIN

Bottlenose dolphins are playful, social and clever creatures! These speedy sea creatures can swim at over 30 kilometres per hour and communicate with each other using a variety of noises, including clicks and whistles.

Dolphins use echolocation to see where objects are. They use their clicking sound to do this. Bottlenose dolphins can make up to one thousand clicks per second!

Female dolphins are called cows,
males are called bulls and young dolphins
are called calves.

There are over 35 species of dolphin of all
different sizes – they range from one and half
to almost ten metres in length!

The blowhole on the top of a
dolphin's head helps it breathe.

PLAYFUL SEA LIONS

Sea lions, like dolphins, are social creatures. In the wild, they can live for around ten to fifteen years.

Female sea lions weigh up to 115 kilograms and can grow to around two metres in length. Male sea lions can weigh up to 450 kilograms and grow to around three metres.

Sea lions are rarely found alone. A group of sea lions on land is known as a colony. When they're in the water, it's called a raft.

Sea lions' bodies are perfectly designed for being in the water. Their smooth torpedo-shaped bodies and powerful fins mean they're quick through the water and can reach speeds of up to 40 kilometres per hour. They can also walk on all four of their flippers!

ORCAS

Orcas are sometimes known as killer whales
but they are actually a type of dolphin.

In the wild orcas can live for around
fifty to ninety years.

Orcas are one of the largest and most
powerful creatures in the ocean and they are
at the top of the food chain – there are no
animals that hunt them.

Orcas weigh up to 5,500 kilograms (roughly the weight of three cars!) and they eat around 227 kilograms of food a day.

Orcas work together in a pod to hunt seals, fish, sharks and octopuses, among other animals, and they can swim at speeds of 48 kilometres per hour.

FIN-TASTICALLY FUNNY JOKES

Coralie loves telling jokes to her friends!
Here are some sea-themed jokes that are
shore to make you laugh… Can you think
of any others?

Why did the fish cross the sea?
To get to the other tide.

Why don't crabs like to share?
Because they're shellfish!

What does a dolphin say when its confused?
Can you please be more Pacific?

What does seaweed say when it's stuck
at the bottom of the sea?
Kelp! Kelp!

Where does a killer whale go for braces?
To the orca-dontist.

What do dolphins need to stay healthy?
Vitamin Sea!

Why are there fish at the bottom of the sea?
Because they dropped out of school.

Why does it take pirates so long
to learn the alphabet?
Because they spend years at C!

How do a group of dolphins make a decision?
They flipper coin!

Why did the lobster blush?
Because the sea weed.

JOIN CORALIE AND HER
FRIENDS FOR THEIR
NEXT ADVENTURE IN...

Mermaids ROCK

The Ice Giant

COMING SOON!

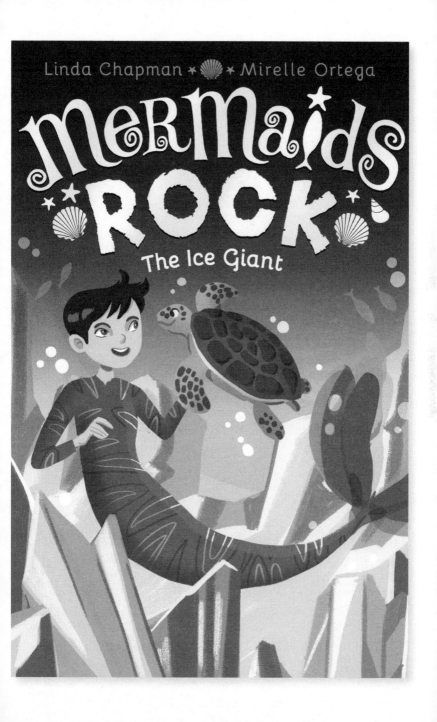

Linda Chapman ★ 🐚 ★ Mirelle Ortega

MERMAiDS
ROCK
The Ice Giant

Chapter One
Turtle Tricks

"Roll over, Tommy!" Kai said hopefully.

Tommy, Kai's hawksbill sea turtle, cocked his head to one side, his dark eyes puzzled.

"Look, watch me, Tommy. When I say roll over, you do this." Kai flicked the end of his red tail and rolled over and over in the warm turquoise water. "Now you try. Roll over and keep going until I say stop. Go on!"

Tommy turned on to his back, pulled his head inside his gold-and-brown shell and stuck his stubby flippers straight up.

"No! That's playing dead," Kai said in frustration. He pushed a hand through his thick dark hair. He'd been trying to teach Tommy to roll over for an hour now. It was the Spring Fair in just over a week and this year there was going to be a contest for the most talented pet. Kai really wanted to enter Tommy so he was trying to teach him some tricks.

Just then a mergirl with a silvery-green tail came over. She had a little gold-and-yellow seahorse with her. Its tail was curled round a lock of her thick brown hair. "Hi, Kai. How's it going?" she asked as Tommy righted himself and swam up to say hello. He nuzzled her with his armoured head.

"It's not going well at all, Marina," admitted Kai as Marina gently scratched under Tommy's chin. Kai and Marina had been friends ever since Marina had moved to Mermaids Rock with her father a few months ago. "Tommy just doesn't seem to want to learn any tricks.

So far I've tried teaching him to shake flippers, play dead and roll over and he's not doing any of them when I ask, even though I know he can do them."

He suddenly realized that, although Marina was usually chatty and smiley, today she looked upset. "Are you OK?" he asked.

Marina shook her head. "No. Not really. It's my dad. He—"

She was interrupted by a sneering laugh. "Are you seriously trying to teach that brainless turtle tricks, Kai Stormchaser? I don't know why you're bothering. You've got no chance in the pet talent contest!"

Kai swung round. Glenda Seaglass, a mergirl with long blond hair, was watching them with her two friends, Jazeela and Racquel. Kai liked almost everyone who lived on the reef but not Glenda – she was as mean as a viperfish.

"Tommy's not brainless!" Marina protested.

"No, he's very clever," said Kai loyally.

"Oh, really?" said Glenda. "Let's see then."
She swam over to the turtle. "Roll over! Go
on!" she commanded.

Tommy thought for a moment and then
offered her a flipper.

Glenda and her friends sniggered. "Oh, yes,
very clever," said Glenda. "I don't think!"

"He's got about as much brain as a jellyfish,"
sneered Racquel.

"Just like Kai!" added Glenda.

The three mergirls squealed with unkind
laughter.

"Oh, go away," Marina said angrily as Kai
hugged Tommy, hoping his feelings weren't
hurt. "It's not like you're taking part in the
talented-pet competition, Glenda. You haven't
even got one!"

"Oh, haven't I?" Glenda smirked. "Shows
how much you know, Marina Silverfin. My
father's getting me a pet – a really *fin-tastic*
one – so all of you in your little Save the Sea

Creatures Club had better watch out. My new pet is going to win and no one else will have a chance. Come on," she said to Jazeera and Racquel. "Let's leave these two losers to their terrible turtle training."

They giggled and swam off.

"Ignore them," Marina said to Tommy. "You're brilliant."

Kai nodded. "They're the brainless ones." He scratched Tommy's head and Tommy waggled a back flipper in delight.

"I feel really sorry for whatever poor pet Glenda gets," said Marina.

"I don't understand how she thinks she might win," said Kai, puzzled. "Even if she gets a new pet, she won't have time to train it before the contest. There's only a week to go."

"You'll have to make sure you beat her," Marina said firmly.

Collect them all and dive into Mermaids Rock!

About the Author

Linda Chapman is the best-selling
author of over 200 books. The biggest
compliment Linda can receive is for a
child to tell her they became a reader
after reading one of her books.
Linda lives in a cottage with a tower in
Leicestershire with her husband, three
children, three dogs and two ponies.
When she's not writing, Linda likes to
ride, read and visit schools and libraries
to talk to people about writing.

www.lindachapmanauthor.co.uk

About the Illustrator

Mirelle Ortega is a Mexican artist based in Los Angeles. She has a MFA in Visual Development from the Academy of Art University in San Francisco. Mirelle loves magic, vibrant colours and ghost stories. But more than anything, she loves telling unique stories with funny characters and a touch of magical realism.

www.mirelleortega.com